Dear Parents:

W9-BDY-416

Congratulations! Your child is taking the first steps on an exciting journey. The destination? Independent reading!

STEP INTO READING® will help your child get there. The program offers five steps to reading success. Each step includes fun stories and colorful art or photographs. In addition to original fiction and books with favorite characters, there are Step into Reading Non-Fiction Readers, Phonics Readers and Boxed Sets, Sticker Readers, and Comic Readers—a complete literacy program with something to interest every child.

Learning to Read, Step by Step!

Ready to Read   Preschool–Kindergarten
• big type and easy words • rhyme and rhythm • picture clues
For children who know the alphabet and are eager to begin reading.

Reading with Help   Preschool–Grade 1
• basic vocabulary • short sentences • simple stories
For children who recognize familiar words and sound out new words with help.

Reading on Your Own   Grades 1–3
• engaging characters • easy-to-follow plots • popular topics
For children who are ready to read on their own.

Reading Paragraphs   Grades 2–3
• challenging vocabulary • short paragraphs • exciting stories
For newly independent readers who read simple sentences with confidence.

Ready for Chapters   Grades 2–4
• chapters • longer paragraphs • full-color art
For children who want to take the plunge into chapter books but still like colorful pictures.

STEP INTO READING® is designed to give every child a successful reading experience. The grade levels are only guides; children will progress through the steps at their own speed, developing confidence in their reading. The F&P Text Level on the back cover serves as another tool to help you choose the right book for your child.

Remember, a lifetime love of reading starts with a single step!

For all the new adventurers,
in kindergarten and beyond
—C.H. & E.T.

For my kindergarten teacher, Ms. Obermeyer,
who commented on my report card:
"Debbie is a leader and has been a positive
role model for other students, with the one
exception of that one day where she had the
whole class drawing on the walls."
—D.P.

Text copyright © 2018 by Cathy Hapka and Ellen Titlebaum
Cover art and interior illustrations copyright © 2018 by Debbie Palen

All rights reserved. Published in the United States by Random House Children's Books,
a division of Penguin Random House LLC, New York.

Step into Reading, Random House, and the Random House colophon are registered trademarks
of Penguin Random House LLC.

Visit us on the Web!
StepIntoReading.com
rhcbooks.com

Educators and librarians, for a variety of teaching tools, visit us at RHTeachersLibrarians.com

Library of Congress Cataloging-in-Publication Data is available upon request.

ISBN 978-1-5247-1551-9 (trade) — ISBN 978-1-5247-1552-6 (lib. bdg.) —
ISBN 978-1-5247-1553-3 (ebook)

Printed in the United States of America
10 9 8 7 6 5 4 3 2 1

This book has been officially leveled by using the F&P Text Level Gradient™ Leveling System.

Random House Children's Books supports the First Amendment and celebrates the right to read.

STEP INTO READING®

2 STEP
READING WITH HELP

How to Start Kindergarten

by Cathy Hapka and Ellen Titlebaum
illustrated by Debbie Palen

Random House 🏠 New York

I am Steve.

I like to beat
my big brother, Will,
at baseball.

We see a new kid.

"Hi! Who are you?"

I ask.

"I am David," he says.

"We just moved here."

I show David
the way to school.
"Will I fit in?"
David asks.
"For sure," I say.
"Just do what I do
and you will be great."

After school,

David and I walk home.

"You were right,"

David says.

"I want to be
just like you!"
"For sure," I agree.
I am an awesome friend!

The next day, David
dresses like I do.
"Nice shirt," I say.
"For sure," David says.

At lunch, David has
a pickle sandwich.
"You eat those, too?" I ask.
"For sure," David says.

From then on, David acts just like me.
I build a tall tower.
David does, too.

I cheer for Will.

David does, too.

14

Having a twin sounds fun.

But it is not.

"David is trying

to be just like me,"

I tell Will.

Will grins.

"Now you know how I feel."

I am the best
at the high bar.

"Look at me," David says.

He is upside down, too!

I cannot take it anymore.

"Stop copying me!"

I yell.

The next day, David and I
do not sit together.

"We will do a dance
at assembly tomorrow,"
Mrs. K says.

"One of you will do
a cartwheel at the end,"
Mrs. K tells us.
"Who wants to do it?"
"I do!" everyone yells.

We have tryouts.

I look to see

how David is doing.

Oops!

I mess up a little.

David wins the solo!

"That solo
should have been mine,"
I tell Will later.
"Why?" Will says.
"It sounds like David's
cartwheel was better."
Big brothers just
do not get it.

The next day,
we wait backstage.
David rushes over.

"I cannot do this!

Too many people are here!

You do the cartwheel

instead."

This is my big chance!

Then I see David's face.

He looks sad.

"You can do it," I say.

"For sure!"

I am right!
David does
an awesome
cartwheel.

"Thanks, Steve,"
David says later.

"You are the
best friend ever!"
"For sure!" I agree.